Disney

my first baby animals Bedtime storybook

Disney PRESS
Los Angeles • New York

First Hardcover Edition, January 2022
10 9 8 7 6 5 4 3 2 1

ISBN 978-1-368-05553-6

FAC-025393-21281

Library of Congress Control Number: 2021934178
Printed in China

For more Disney Press fun, visit www.disneybooks.com

Contents

This book belongs to:

Disney

THE ARISTOCATS

The Birthday Wish

"Good night, my loves," Duchess said to her three kittens, Marie, Berlioz, and Toulouse.

"Sleep tight, kiddos," O'Malley said as he TUCKED IN THE KITTENS.

"*Please* may I go to the party tonight?" Marie asked.

Duchess shook her head. "You need a good night's sleep."

Voices and music drifted from downstairs. Duchess and O'Malley were throwing A BIRTHDAY PARTY for their friend Scat Cat.

Marie sighed. Oh, how she wished she were allowed to join them! Scat Cat was her friend, too!

Marie came up with a great plan. She could sneak into the party if she looked like an adult.

She found the PERFECT DISGUISE. Marie thought she looked very grown-up.

She crept into the parlor and looked around. Scat Cat was leading the band in a JAZZ NUMBER. Duchess and O'Malley were chatting with some cats in the corner. But most of the cats were dancing.

Marie wanted to dance, too. But she mustn't get caught.

A lady cat gave Marie a funny look.

"I like your collar," Marie said.

"I like your hat," the cat said. It was working! Marie's disguise was PERFECT.

Later some of the guests played party games. Marie enjoyed the charades, but Pin the Tail on the Doggie was her **FAVORITE**. She won every round.

As Marie removed her blindfold, the band started playing a new tune. Scat Cat put down his trumpet.

"You're on your own, fellas!" he said to the band. "This birthday cat has got a date with the dance floor." Scat Cat walked over to Marie. "Ma'am," he said with a wink, "**MAY I HAVE THIS DANCE**?"

Marie forgot all about getting in trouble. She went out onto the dance floor with Scat Cat.

"Enjoying the party, Marie?" Scat Cat asked. "Don't worry. Your secret is safe with me. Let's just dance!"

Marie whirled around, and her disguise went **FLYING OFF**!

"MARIE!"

The music stopped, and everyone stared. Marie's mother was marching right toward her!

"Young lady, you are supposed to be in bed!" Duchess said.

Marie looked up sadly. "I'm sorry, Mama," she said.

"Say, Duchess, it *is* my birthday," Scat Cat said. "How about letting her stay? It's my BIRTHDAY WISH!" Then he blew out the candles on his cake.

"Well, just this once, I suppose. But you're going to bed early tomorrow night, Marie. Understood?"

Marie nodded. "Thank you, Mama! I promise I'll never sneak out again."

Marie stayed at the party, singing and dancing and talking with the grown-ups. Finally, it was time for everyone to go home, and Duchess carried a very sleepy Marie up to bed.

Marie would never forget her SPECIAL NIGHT and Scat Cat's birthday wish!

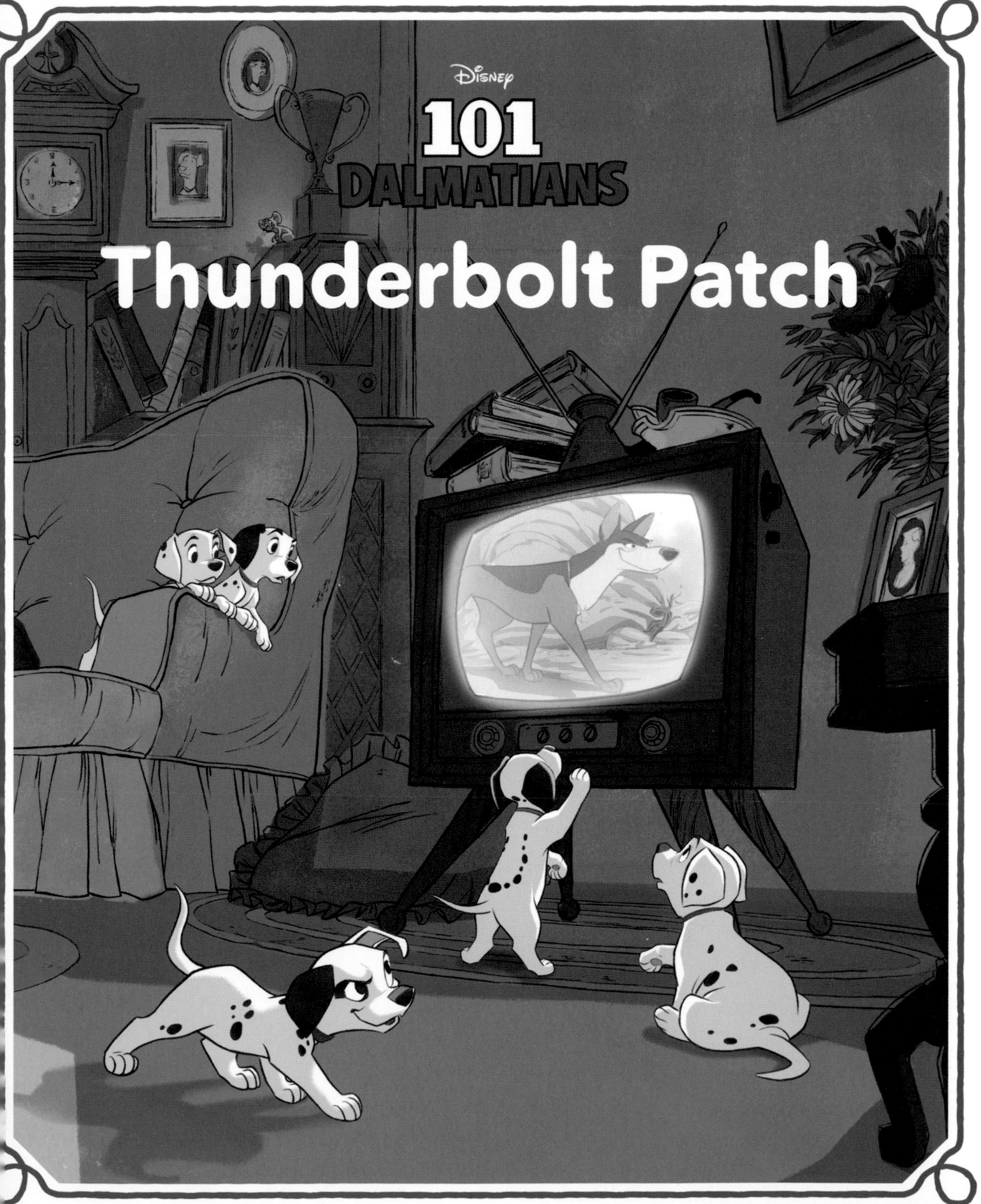
Disney
101
DALMATIANS
Thunderbolt Patch

One evening, Pongo, Perdita, and their fifteen Dalmatian puppies gathered around the television to watch the heroic adventures of **THUNDERBOLT THE DOG**.

When the show ended, Pongo and Perdita set about putting their puppies to bed.

All the puppies settled into bed—except for Patch. Patch wanted to go on an **ADVENTURE**, like Thunderbolt.

When the puppies heard a strange scurrying sound nearby, Patch knew it was his chance.

The puppies scampered out of bed and snuck upstairs after the fearsome outlaw.

"There!" Lucky yelped. "Behind the bin! He's heading for the door!"

But before the puppies could catch the bandit, they heard someone coming up the stairs. It was Nanny! If she caught the puppies out of their bed, they would be in BIG TROUBLE.

"Hide!" Patch whispered.

"Now, what's all this noise?" Nanny asked. But the pups were well hidden.

Patch spied the scoundrel slipping back downstairs.

Once the coast was clear, the pups resumed their chase . . . **TAILS FIRST**. Together, they all slid down the hallway bannister.

"The thief is escaping!" Patch shouted. "After him!"

Patch followed the bandit, and the puppies followed Patch . . . right out the BACK DOOR!

"He's headed toward the courtyard," Patch said. "We can't lose him!" The puppies BOUNDED into the courtyard.

"Catching culprits makes me hungry," Rolly complained.

Lucky for Rolly, at that moment the bandit ran right past the pups . . . and into the kitchen.

The pups raced back inside. "That sly burglar must be in here somewhere," Patch said.

"There he is!" Rolly shouted.

Rolly DARTED toward the bandit . . . but they both suddenly disappeared in a cloud of WHITE DUST.

"That pup doesn't have any spots!" Patch yelled. "He must be the intruder! Get him!"

The puppies all pounced on Rolly together.

In the COMMOTION, the little thief jumped onto the counter and scampered away.

"Mother and Father are here!" Penny shouted. "Everyone back to bed!"

"Come along, chaps!" shouted the leader of the pack. "Thunderbolt Patch will SAVE THE DAY!"

Led by Patch, the pups raced back to their cozy bed.

Pongo and Perdita peeked in on their PRECIOUS puppies. They were all curled up in bed . . . just as their parents had left them.

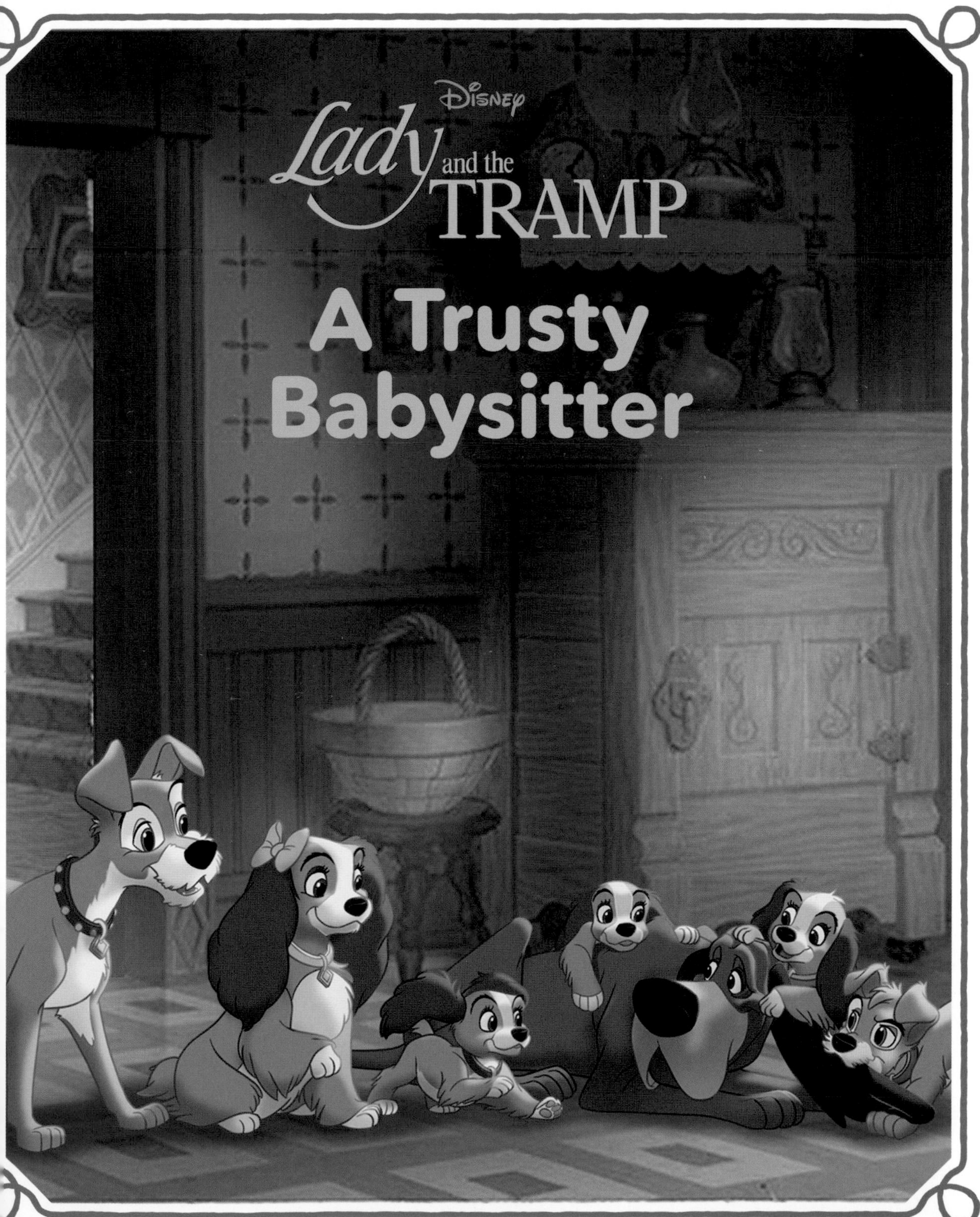
Disney
Lady and the TRAMP
A Trusty Babysitter

It was a BEAUTIFUL EVENING. Lady and Tramp were dressed up for dinner.

Lady was busy making sure their puppies–Scooter, Fluffy, Ruffy, and Scamp–were fed, bathed, and ready to be tucked into bed. "Now, be good for your babysitter," she said.

Just then, a KNOCK sounded at the doggy door.

"Uncle Trusty!" barked the puppies. Wagging their tails, they pounced on him and licked his ears.

"Don't let Scamp give you any trouble," Tramp said.

Lady and Tramp kissed their puppies and headed out the door.

Trusty followed the puppies to the parlor. He began to tell them a bedtime story, but he forgot part of it.

Scooter, Fluffy, and Ruffy YAWNED and CLOSED THEIR EYES.

"Wait one doggone minute," Trusty said as he counted three furry heads. "Weren't there four of you before?"

Scamp was gone!

Trusty put his nose to the floor in search of Scamp's trail. Unfortunately, Trusty's sense of smell had been gone for years. But that didn't stop him. He **SNIFFED** and **SNIFFED**, following his nose . . . straight into the piano!

Slowly, Trusty made his way to the kitchen, which looked as if a storm had just blown through it. There were SMASHED EGGS and SPILLED MILK everywhere!

"I'd say the pup's been here," Trusty said with a sigh.

Scamp wasn't there anymore, but he had left behind a trail of floury paw prints.

Trusty followed the prints into the living room. It looked even worse than the kitchen. Jim Dear's newspaper was in TATTERS, and his slippers were TORN TO SHREDS. Darling's knitting had been unraveled. Yarn crisscrossed the room like a GIANT SPIDERWEB.

Trusty followed the YARN until it led him back into the hall and to the doggy door.

"Scamp?" Trusty called. He noticed a hole at the base of a wooden fence.

"Doggone it! The pup's gone and flown the coop!" he moaned. What was he going to do?

Trusty poked his head through the hole. He saw Lady and Tramp **STROLLING DOWN THE STREET** toward home.

Trusty plodded back into the house and sat by the doggy door to meet the couple and break the bad news to them.

"Trusty!" Tramp said as he and Lady stepped through the door. "HOW DID IT GO?"

Before Trusty could answer, Lady pranced up and kissed his cheek. "Dear Trusty. We really can't thank you enough. Let's go and peek in on the puppies, shall we?"

Trusty hung his head and followed Lady into the parlor, dreading the story he had to tell. How was he going to explain that he had lost Scamp?

Suddenly, Lady turned around. "Trusty!" she said. "However did you do this?"

"DO WHAT?" Trusty asked, confused.

Lady pointed to the puppies' basket. "Why, get Scamp to go to bed, of course. Even we have trouble making him settle down."

"Well, would you look at that," Tramp said, eyeing his son. "Well done, **OLD CHAP**. I'll tell you something: we'll definitely be asking you to babysit again!"

Thumper's Summer Day

One summer morning, the sun had just begun to come up. The CREATURES of the forest were starting to stir.

But THUMPER and his sisters were already wide-awake and ready to play.

As the sun rose higher and higher in the sky, it got warmer and warmer. So the bunnies decided to cool off in the stream.

SPLISH, SPLASH!

Then they HOPPED to a hidden hollow. Inside the hollow, it was cool and dark.

Later, as the sun crept across the sky, Thumper sailed across the pond. He waved HELLO to his beaver friend as he floated by.

The hot summer sun blazed on. The bunnies cloud-gazed as the fluffy shapes moved across the sky.

The bunnies berry-grazed until their TUMMIES were full.

Finally, the sun took a nap. The bunnies hopped and danced as RAIN fell down.

As the sun started to set and the cool breeze of evening began to blow, the BUNNIES had a picnic.

The MOON came out. The sky grew darker. The sun headed home, and so did the bunnies.

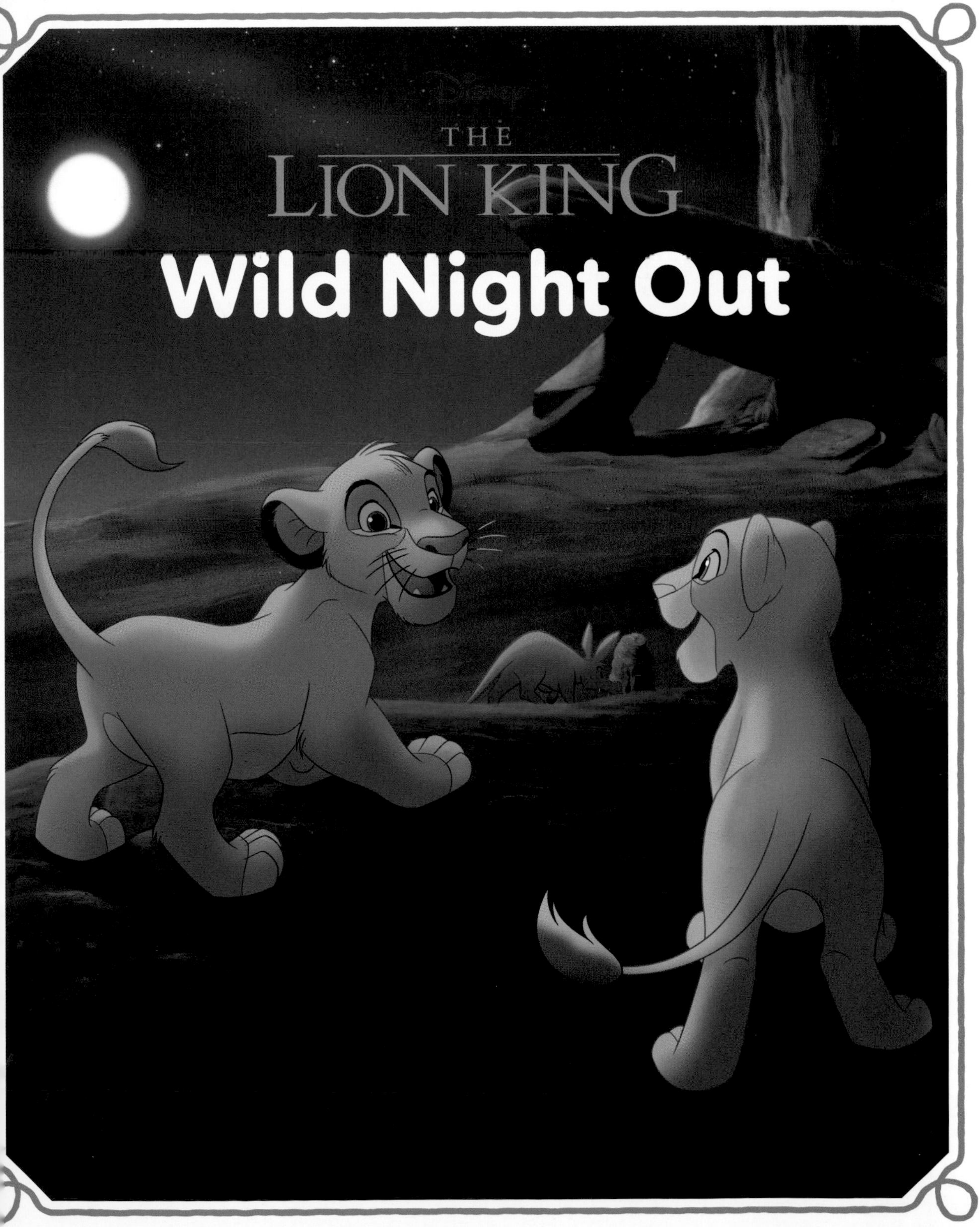

Wild Night Out

It was LATE AT NIGHT in the Pride Lands. In their den, the lions were asleep—except for Simba. He just wasn't tired!

Suddenly, the little prince heard a noise coming from outside. Then he heard it again.

"There's something outside!" Simba said to Nala. "Come on! Don't you want to find out what it is?"

Nala opened her eyes. "**RIGHT NOW?** But it's so dark!"

"Let's go!" Simba said.

Together, Simba and Nala tiptoed past their mothers and the rest of the sleeping pride.

"Look! Over there!" Nala said.

A **SHADOWY FIGURE** shuffled out from behind a tall mound of dirt.

"What is it?" Nala asked.

Simba shrugged.

"Hello!" Simba called. "Hey! You! Over here!" Startled, THE CREATURE looked up.

"Are you lost?" Nala asked. "Why aren't you home in bed?"

"I'm an aardvark," the creature replied. "We sleep during the day and play all night."

The aardvark **TURNED AWAY** and started to waddle off.

"Wait!" Simba called. "Where are you going?"

"To find my friends," the aardvark said. "Do you want to come?"

Without another thought, they bounded after the aardvark.

The cubs hadn't gone far when Simba stepped on something SHARP. A little needle was sticking out of his foot.

"Sorry," someone said. A creature with lots of sharp needles all over his back was behind them. "My needles keep anyone from bothering me," the porcupine said.

The cubs kept chasing after the aardvark and found him talking to a springhare.

The springhare suggested a **JUMPING CONTEST**, and Nala and Simba accepted right away.

One jump into the contest, Simba realized they might have made a mistake. The springhare jumped three times as far as the cubs.

"Are you hungry?" the aardvark asked.

The cubs' STOMACHS GRUMBLED. They weren't used to being up so late after dinner.

But when Simba and Nala saw what the aardvark was eating, they decided maybe they weren't quite so hungry after all.

Suddenly, a cold wind RUFFLED the cubs' fur. Nala and Simba both yawned. The night had been quite an ADVENTURE. They were starting to get tired.

But as Simba looked around, he realized he didn't have any idea where the den was.

"Which way did we come from?" Simba asked.

Nala looked around. "I'm not sure," she said. "It's TOO DARK.

"Wait!" Nala cried. High above them, the clouds had parted, revealing the moon. Its LIGHT SHONE on the path Simba and Nala had been looking for. In the distance, they could see Pride Rock.

The cubs said GOODBYE to their new friend and hurried back home. They saw that everyone was still asleep.

"See you in the morning," Simba said, then paused to yawn. "What's for breakfast, do you think?"

"Anything sounds good," Nala said, "as long as it's not bugs!"

Disney

DUMBO

Dumbo's Snowy Day

One chilly day, the circus animals were on their way to a new town. Their train was struggling to get through the falling snow. The train came to a stop, and everyone waited for the snow to pass.

Dumbo was happy. He'd never played in the snow! Mrs. Jumbo gave him a GENTLE NUZZLE. Soon Dumbo got the hang of walking through the snow.

All morning, Dumbo and his mother played in the SNOW.

Suddenly, Dumbo slid down a steep hill ending in a cliff. When Mrs. Jumbo reached the bottom of the hill, she realized she couldn't get back up!

"You will have to fly off and get help," Mrs. Jumbo told Dumbo.

So off Dumbo flew, as fast as his ears would take him. Dumbo RACED to the train. Quickly, he gathered all the animals together so they could help.

"What are we waiting for?" Timothy Q. Mouse cried. "We've got to save Mrs. Jumbo!"

Dumbo led his friends back to the cliff.

By the time they found Mrs. Jumbo, a windstorm had pushed her even closer to the cliff's edge. The animals had to think of something FAST!

"Oh, dear," said the giraffe. "How can we get down there to help?"

Timothy SNAPPED his fingers. He had an idea. "Everybody line up!" he shouted. He ordered the animals to grab one another's tails. At the front of the line, the ostrich leaned over the cliff above to take hold of Mrs. Jumbo's trunk.

"One, two, three, PULL!" Timothy yelled.

The animals worked together until Mrs. Jumbo made it safely to the top of the cliff. But suddenly, there was a loud CRACK. The cliffside started to give way.

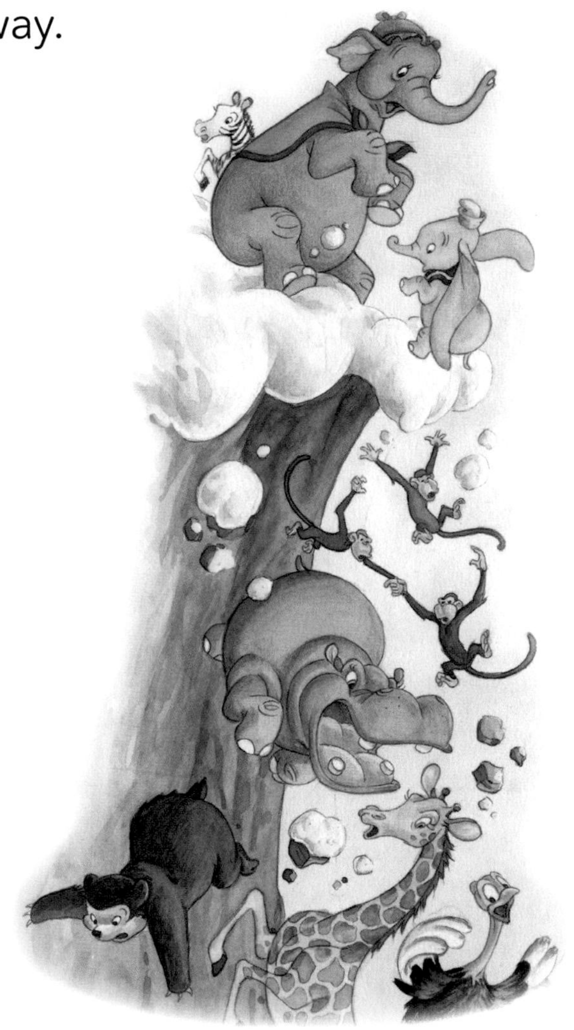

All the animals tumbled together and rolled down the hill. Before long, they had become a giant snowball!

"How do you stop this thing?" Timothy shouted. The animal snowball gathered speed until . . .

. . . it hit the bottom of the hill and broke apart!

"Is everyone okay?" Timothy asked.

Fortunately, everyone was fine—just a little DIZZY from their unexpected snow ride. All the animals began walking back to the train.

That night, Mrs. Jumbo gave Dumbo a warm bath.

"Thank you for flying to find help today," Mrs. Jumbo said.

"Hey! Don't forget about me," said Timothy from his teacup bath. "I helped, too!"

Mrs. Jumbo nodded. "You certainly did. Thank you!"

Then it was time for bed. Dumbo SNUGGLED up against his mother, and Timothy NESTLED underneath Dumbo's ear. Dumbo fell asleep right away. He was glad to be warm and safe with his mother as the snow fell gently outside.